Especially for

Published in Canada by Tundra Books,
75 Sherbourne Street, Toronto, Ontario M5A 2P9

Published in the United States by Tundra Books of Northern New York,
P.O. Box 1030, Plattsburgh, New York 12901

Library of Congress Control Number: 2007902757

LIBRARY AND ARCHIVES CANADA CATALOGUING IN PUBLICATION

Romance, Trisha, 1951-
A star for Christmas / Trisha Romance.

ISBN 978-0-88776-836-1

1. Christmas stories, Canadian (English). I. Title.
PS8635.044S72 2007   JC813'.6   C2007-902333-9

We acknowledge the financial support of the Government of Canada
through the Book Publishing Industry Development Program (BPIDP) and
that of the Government of Ontario through the Ontario Media Development
Corporation's Ontario Book Initiative.
We further acknowledge the support of the Canada Council for the Arts and
the Ontario Arts Council for our publishing program.

ONTARIO ARTS COUNCIL
CONSEIL DES ARTS DE L'ONTARIO

Medium: watercolor on paper

PRINTED IN CANADA

1 2 3 4 5 6   12 11 10 09 08 07

In memory of our beloved pony, Turwynn

For my family

Long ago this story was written on my heart.
At last this is my gift to you.
May God's light continue to shine on you
as brightly as the Star over Bethlehem.

And for "Star,"
the endearing little reindeer
that I met, once upon a time...
because, after all,
a promise is a promise.

God Bless You This Christmas
and Always

xo

Once upon a time, there was a little house of
wood and stone at the edge of a quiet meadow.
You might think that it had always been there,
but that was not so.

There was a time when only the animals of the forest
lived among the great pine and birch trees surrounding
the meadow. One of them was a little orphaned reindeer.

In the village not far away was a carpenter, a woodsman, who had spent many years lovingly crafting homes for the townsfolk. The time had come to build a house of his own, a place to share all the joys of his heart, a home.

And so, on a winter's day, he hiked to the peaceful meadow and began to clear his land at the forest edge. An old abandoned cabin nearby became his workshop.

Soon, all of this activity attracted the curious little reindeer. It wasn't long before the two became inseparable friends. The carpenter named him Little Star because his company brightened the darkest of winter days.

Long into the spring and throughout the endless hot days of summer, the carpenter worked until he grew weary. But in the golden days of autumn, just when it seemed impossible to have a home in time for Christmas, he heard the happy sound of voices ringing in the frosty air. One by one, the villagers had heard about the carpenter's house, and they arrived to help.

The carpenter's heart was overjoyed at the sight of them. "Come in! Come in, my dear ones," he called. "Bless you. What a wonderful feast you've brought today!"

The warmth of their company was as warm as their soup. The villagers loved to hear the carpenter's stories of faith, hope, and love, but when the first snowflakes of the season began to fall, all thoughts and words turned to one thing – Christmas!

Though it was sad to say good-bye, everyone knew that soon they would return, for there was much work to be done before Christmas Eve. "Won't you be lonely?" the youngest one asked.

With smiling eyes, the carpenter answered, "Don't worry. I'm not alone. Does the moon feel lonely in a sky full of stars? Besides, I have a bright little star to keep me company!"

After the visitors had gone, the carpenter worked long
into the night, by moonlight and lantern light, while
Little Star slept soundly in his stall. With Christmas
coming, the carpenter had many gifts to carve. But this
year, there was one very important surprise to finish.

At last, with the setting of the moon, the workshop
grew quiet. While Kitty purred on her feather bed and
the embers glowed in the hearth, it was time for
peaceful slumber under a rooftop covered in snow.

As the days grew shorter, the Christmas surprise
drew closer and closer to being finished.

Week by week, with the help of many hands, the house finally became a home. After his belongings had found their rightful place, the carpenter stood quietly for a moment and looked around. There was just one thing missing.

The next morning, surrounded by excited children, the carpenter hitched up Little Star. They were off to the woods in search of the perfect Christmas tree. And find the perfect one, they did! After Little Star received his reward, they were back on the path home, eager to decorate the magnificent tree.

They just had to *SQUEEZE* it through the door first!

To everyone's delight, steaming cocoa was waiting on the stone hearth. But nothing warmed them like the lighting of the Christmas tree. When it had been trimmed with yards of paper chains, popcorn garlands, and glittering stars, the carpenter stood back and declared, "This is the best Christmas tree ever!"

All too soon, the evening passed and the carpenter said, "Now, my dears, it's time to run along, for tomorrow is Christmas Eve, and we all must get some rest."

As the spicy scent of the Christmas tree filled the room and Kitty curled up in his arms, the carpenter felt content. Within moments, they were asleep in the warmth of his cozy chair.

Tomorrow was only a dream away.

In the morning, the carpenter rose early. After a breakfast
of warm porridge, he read aloud from his well-worn
Bible, just as he had always done. But this day's passage
was special. It told of the night that Jesus was born. Even
Kitty seemed to understand as the carpenter read, "When
they saw the star, they rejoiced with exceeding great joy."

The woods were silent in the crisp early morning as
the carpenter and Little Star headed up the trail to put
the finishing touches on the Christmas Eve surprise.

At last Christmas Eve arrived, and with it, the treasured friends whose love had built this wonderful home.

The savory food and the Christmas sweets they brought made the table groan, but before the feast began, they all joined hands. In a soft voice, the carpenter graciously thanked everyone for their boundless friendship. Then he gave thanks to God for this blessed Christmas Eve.

When the merry feast was over, a little one asked shyly, "Is it true? Will there be a special Christmas surprise tonight?"

The carpenter whispered, "Shall we go and see?"

All bundled up, and
with lanterns in hand,
they followed Little Star
and the carpenter into
the snowy woods.

Before long, they came to a grotto of rocks and arching
birch trees, glowing warmly in the night. As they drew
closer, they wondered at the beauty before them.

There, lying softly in a manger, was Baby Jesus.
Beside Him, kneeling in the golden straw, was Mary,
His mother, and Joseph, His earthly father. With loving
care, the carpenter had carved each figure from wood.
He had sanded them until they gleamed and painted
them with an artist's touch. Those gathered were filled
with "exceeding great joy."

While the children knelt to get a closer look, the carpenter reached into his jacket for his Bible. In the calm stillness, as he read about the night that Jesus was born, snowflakes began to fall like millions of stars from the heavens above.

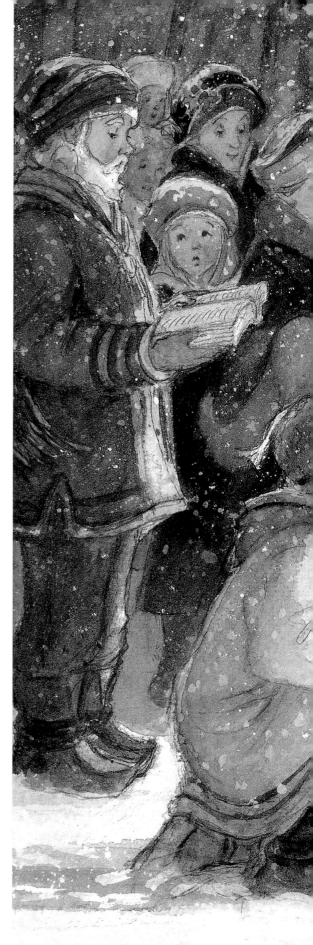

The hour was growing late, and it was time for the
parents to take their sleepy children home. Although the
carpenter had given each of the young ones a handmade
gift from his workshop, the Baby Jesus in the woods
was the gift they would treasure in their hearts forever.

As the sleigh whisked them back to their homes in the
village, the children couldn't wait to open their gift from
the beloved carpenter. Inside the brown-paper package
was Little Star, hand-carved and painted with great love.
Tucked inside the bed of fine straw was a message:

"GOD BLESS YOU THIS CHRISTMAS
AND ALWAYS. *xo*"